W9-AXA-893

I am an ARO PUBLISHING
TEN WORD BOOK

My ten words are:

where	do
we	find
snails	whales
money	honey
in	books

Library Bear

10 WORDS

Story and Pictures by Bob Reese

Where
do
we
find,

Snails?

Where
do
we
find,

Whales?

Where do we find,

Money?

Where
do
we
find,

Honey?

In
books!

In snail books.
In whale books.
In money books.
In honey books.
In books.